Broken Silence

Broken Silence

Valerie M. Davis

Copyright © 2018 by Valerie M. Davis.

ISBN: Softcover   978-1-9845-6758-1
           eBook   978-1-9845-6757-4

All rights reserved. No part of this book may be reproduced or transmitted in any form or by any means, electronic or mechanical, including photocopying, recording, or by any information storage and retrieval system, without permission in writing from the copyright owner.

Any people depicted in stock imagery provided by Getty Images are models, and such images are being used for illustrative purposes only. Certain stock imagery © Getty Images.

Print information available on the last page.

Rev. date: 11/16/2018

To order additional copies of this book, contact:
Xlibris
1-888-795-4274
www.Xlibris.com
Orders@Xlibris.com
785010

To my husband, Donny, thank you for being you and loving me. To our children, thank you for understanding...eventually! And knowing that my love for you is purely unconditional.

OMG! You are such a strong woman. I hear that often by so many different people. I always reply with a simple, "Thank you" but inside I'm secretly choking a booger out of their nose. Now, don't get me wrong I love being recognized for the things I do for others while going through so much, but sometimes I just wish someone would hold me and tell me it's okay not to be strong. Does that even make sense? Maybe I should take you back to when I was a little girl. I'm not THAT old so it won't take too long...

"You get a right to tell your story and the fact that somebody might be embarrassed is not your business- it's theirs." - Unknown

Growing up is a blur for me. It wasn't "fun". I felt like an only child because my siblings were so much older than me. I remember adult parties, my dad driving us home drunk, and my mom working as a nurse but also drinking a lot. There was a lot of fighting between my parents inside of that house. I feared my dad. I never verbally asked him for anything, I always wrote a note if I needed anything especially money. My parents didn't really allow me to go off the porch to play. When I think back now, we were no better than anyone else on that block.

I was enrolled in a Head Start, but we had close family friends that lived near us. I remember one of our family friends would always play with me until someone picked me up. I'm not sure when it started, I had to be 3 or 4 because I was not in school all day. Anyway, one day he had me undress down to my underwear and then sat me on top of his bed. They lived in a 2 flat also but they never rented out their second floor. I remember he told me if I told anyone what was about to happen I would get a whooping. He pulled down his pants and underwear and put his penis in my mouth. I remember feeling like I was going to choke or throw up. I remember him pushing my head back and forth until he ejaculated. He made me swallow it. I was told to put my clothes back on and we went back downstairs. I don't know how long this went on but thinking about it now, it seemed like forever. One day we were up there and his sister came upstairs and walked in his room. She yelled at him asking him what he was doing and I remember her helping me with my overalls and rushing me downstairs. She told their mother what she saw and I can still see their mother whacking him over and over with a broom. I don't remember how I got home that day, I just remember I didn't ever go back there. No one told me it was wrong. No one told me it was not my fault. No one asked how I felt. No one asked if I was ok. No one told me what he did was NOT okay. No one.

"If you never heal from what hurt you, you'll bleed on people who didn't cut you." - Unknown

I went to Public School for kindergarten, Catholic School for grades 1-2, Private School for grades 3-8 and Public School for all four years of high school. I never thought I was pretty, still don't. The boys used to make fun of my big forehead and glasses. I hated school. I had 3 friends at school and friends that lived next door to me. I loved to play barbies and color. I was allowed to have friends sleepover but I wasn't ever really allowed to sleepover at anyone's house. No one at home talked about sex or what happened to me. My sister ended up moving out and I began to spend the weekends at her place. I loved being around my sister.

My dad was my hero. I just never understood why he didn't protect me from that boy. At some point my mom became close with a lady who lived close to us. She had three daughters and two sons they were all older than me. I was allowed to spend the night once and I remember one of the girls, fingering me. I remember the boy trying to penetrate me. I did not sleep at all that night. I could not wait to be picked up the following day so i could go home and sleep in my own bed. I said no when asked to spend the night after that. I'm not sure how old I was.

Before high school my moms drinking got worse and so did the physical altercations between her and my dad. I remember my dad beating my mother with a wire hanger. He ran a hot bath afterwards and forced her into the tub and forced her head under the water. He held it under the water briefly but at that moment it seemed like an eternity. I was always told to go into my room but I would creep out when it seemed quiet. I believe my sister was either married or living with her husband at that time and my brothers were away at college. My father worked for the Post Office and my mom was a LPN. I was able to walk to neighborhood liquor store called, *Personnel Liquor Store* as young as 10 years old and pick up beer for my mother. She would call ahead and speak with the owner, Jerry, the owner, and I would give him the money and he would give me the beer. Sometimes it was very late or at least dark out. I've never liked the smell of beer from an early age.

Don't get me wrong, it wasn't all bad. We would go out to eat a lot and my dad loved to cook. I was a picky eater so he would always fix me something that I liked to eat. He never told me he loved me until November of 1988. I knew he loved me, he just never said it verbally. I knew he loved my mom, he hated the person she became after drinking. My dad was a smoker and he was a social drinker, he liked Crown Royal. He enjoyed to gamble - horses, bingo, dogs, and then the lottery when it started. He was a deacon at our church and he helped start a food co-op. He also worked with Habitat for Humanity. We drove by what used to be Maywood Race Track today. I never understood the method of his madness but when he won he won big. I remember when he won huge and paid off the mortgage to our building. He burned it over an astray at the dining room table. He always took care of home first, and then he would take a trip with my mom. They went to Spain, Africa, Vegas often and Mardi Gras almost every year.

As I am writing I realize a lot of things are a blur. I remember visits to my grandmas house. There were early Saturday morning drives to the south side of Chicago to visit my dad's uncles, and road trips to my brothers graduations. We also drove down to Humboldt, TN whenever there was a family reunion or a funeral. Road trips were cool because there was no drinking or fighting. Just Ray Charles on 8 track tape, over and over again for eight hours……..

My dad was a wonderful, hardworking family man. He was also a foster child. His mom died when he was 2 years old and my mother found his dad in 1970, the year I was born. I was told a few years ago that his own aunt that raised him (his grandmother's sister) was mean to him. He was eventually kidnapped by his mom's brothers and taken to St. Louis, Missouri. He was being raised in Humboldt, Tennessee at the time and eventually returned, My dad didn't know how to verbally express love but I knew he loved me. The night my father suffered his massive heart attack, my best friend and I were trying to figure out if we wanted to go by my sisters or stay in. It was a Friday the 13th. My daddy was in for the night and said I could use the car. My mom called while we were there and told me I needed to come home because my daddy was sick. We rushed home and there was an ambulance blocking the street in front of our house. I just stood numb on the porch. It was so cold and they worked on him out there for a long time. My mom, a nurse, said he was complaining of indigestion. He had decided to try Taco Bell for the first time that night. She said he kept feeling like he needed to use the bathroom, and that's when she knew it was a heart attack and called 911. They told us his heart stopped twice in the ambulance. He ended up having a triple bypass as a result. If only he had stopped smoking. He told me for the 1st time, after his heart attack, he loved me. I was 16. They gave him 24 hours to live and I was in the ICU visiting him. He motioned for me to come closer to him. He told me to kiss him on his forehead and he said he loved me and if anything happened to him make sure that I took care of my mother.

Let's jump forward to those private schools days. Horrible. The only thing that brought me joy was chapel on Thursdays and basketball (that apparently my family knows nothing about SMH). I was picked up by the school van so my day started at 6 am because I was picked up first. Ugh! It's probably why I'm not a morning person now. The other kids on the block went to school together had breaks together and many of them are still friends to this day. Oh well. Private school was overrated. I appreciate developing a relationship with the Lord at such a young age, learning how to pray, and the feeling of family that was present on Sundays when we attended church. I remember my 8th grade graduation class was the largest (at that time) at Bethel. It was 13 of us. That was pretty cool. I loved our basketball team - Bethel Blazers. I was a point guard but we have no pictures so no one believes I even played. It's funny at time but it's hurtful at times too because I loved it and learned a lot about friendship, trust, and teamwork. Oh well...

    I couldn't wait to go to high school. I was accepted into Von Steuben Metropolitan Science Center. My brother Phillip had also went there. I looked at it as a chance to be around "normal" kids. You know public school kids. There were a few of us from Bethel that would be headed way up on the north-side everyday with the commute being between 1-1 1/2 hours depending on the day, weather or whatever surprises CTA had in store for us on any given day. I made friends fast. There was nothing that interest me- extracurricular wise. I wanted to play basketball but when tryouts came it was nothing like basketball at in grammar school. I was the best defensive player then. At the tryouts I was a small 100 pound girl in a gym full of athletes. I didn't try. I look back as I write and I realize I defeated myself at a very early age all from allowing someone to take my voice, my truth, my power at 3 or 4 years old (powerful revelation).

    Anyway, I fell for a guy in high school. I fell hard. He was the total opposite of me or so he seemed to be. He was popular, funny, full of energy, talented, and the class clown. I'm not sure how long we dated. It might have been until the new fresh "meat" came in our sophomore year and he picked someone else. When we broke up we promised each other we would go to our Senior Prom together even if we were dating someone else, and we did. During 10-12 grade I tried dating but I wasn't really into it. I ended up dating this Puerto Rican guy and he turned into a stalker. My funniest memory of him was our birthdays which were both in August. He helped plan my surprise 16th birthday party. We were broken up by the time the party arrived. It was a good turn out, but I was happy when it was over :).

    I took Driver's Ed my 10th grade year and was driving to school in whatever car I could use, at that time. I met my best friend the summer of junior year I believe. She was my true friend. We were both the baby of the family, and her siblings had also went to Von. I was always able to be myself around her and her family. The highlight of our day was getting the keys and going to Walgreens. LMAO. Sounds lame now but we were out of trouble. My junior year is a blur. Not sure why at this time. I'm sure it will come back to me. I know I was interested in a boy from our neighborhood at the time. Another total opposite. He was cool. He was a ball player and going to be tall. I think I always felt he was kind of immature and only wanted one thing. During that time my sister was married with 3 kids and moved into a house on the north side of the city and closer to my first boyfriend (Yay -_-) We were never good together. They call it friends with benefits now. I spent summer of my Junior Year living with my sister and brother-in-law, babysitting while they went to work to make some money. I was pretty much a live-in nanny and the money was awesome at that age. My goal for senior year was to get in and get the hell out. I took zero period gym and was home everyday in time to catch my soap opera, "One Life to Live". Prom colors were picked during the first semester, grey +

light pink. Did I mention we were in the same division (home room) all 4 years? That means I had to interact with him everyday.

Despite the fact that he was in a serious relationship with an underclassmen at this point, my ex-sweetheart and I were still planning our prom. Our conversations started and ended in homeroom. My brother in law was set to rent the car, and he'd pick me up from my house. Now that I think about it, it wasn't as much of a big deal as it is these days. My parents and sister were there along with my best friend/neighbor. My dress came out perfect, a lady from my church made it. Prom was at a hotel downtown. It wasn't what I expected, I don't even recall us dancing but I know he mingled. He was crowned Prom King and a girl I can't remember was crowned Queen. The Prom theme was "I had theTime of My Life" the song from the movie Dirty Dancing, and we were given memorabilia with our H.S name and class on a glass champagne flute. He was driving so reckless when we left that our glasses broke in the back seat, that's when it hit me that the whole thing had been a bad idea. I didn't go to Great America the next day. He went with his girlfriend. Looking back on it, I wish I had went with my neighbor. I probably would have had fun. All in all, senior year was fun. I liked the freedom that came along with almost being done with school. I was so excited for Graduation. My sister was in charge of taking pictures. I found out later, that after she snapped the first picture the film rewound and she didn't know that meant the film needed to be changed. So, now I have no pictures... it's funny NOW. My parents were there, they were late because my mom was drinking that day.

I think when it came down to making the decision about going to college, I didn't have an option. It was expected. Both of my brothers went and graduated and my sister went to a community college but ended up taking a Certification Business Course. I had never had a job outside of babysitting but I knew I didn't want to work with children. I had no clue what I wanted to be when I grew up. As a little girl I wanted to be the first black President of the United States. That summer seemed to fly by, I was dreading going back to school, but I wanted to be away from home - the drinking, the fighting, the unhappiness.

Eventually I decided to attend Aurora University especially since I only scored a 16 on the ACT and that was good enough for them. The day my daddy took me to the bank to sign my loan papers I should have spoke up and said I didn't want to go, and picked up a trade or just got a job. I wanted to go to the Police Academy, but he said no, it was too dangerous. I spent time with my best friend as much as possible. She was going to Western Illinois University.

When I went to school, it was a 45 minute drive and I knew who my roommate would be before I arrived. Underclassmen arrived first and the weekend was supposed to be for incoming freshman and their families but my parents helped my unpack, then left. There were a few upperclassmen there and they'd ask who my roommate was and I'd say her name, they'd call her "microwave". That was because she was known for burning guys (giving them STDS).

School started off cool, I ended up being a couple of doors away from a girl I went to church with. I went home practically every weekend on the Amtrak train. Sometimes my mom would let me take her car for the week. I eventually met a guy from New York and we started dating. I stayed in an all girl dorm but he would sneak and spend the night but the RA (Resident Assistant) was eventually told he was spotted coming out of my room so I was given a verbal warning. As the first semester went on I just stopped going to class and eventually had to leave. My dad was very disappointed. When I came home from school it wasn't as bad as I thought. My dad told me he wished I had told him I wanted to take a break instead of going away for nothing. The thing is, I didn't want to be in **that house**, but I understood what he was trying to say. My sister and her husband had purchased a house far out south by this time. My mother was a visiting nurse, she would go see patients the day after they had eye surgery. My father worked nights at the post office. Since I was home he would come in from work in the mornings and take her to visit patients on the south side and I would take her to visit patients on the west side. I learned how to get around the city pretty well and to this day my daughter is amazed that if she gives me an address I can tell her the cross streets.

This driving my mom around thing was "ok" I mean it was the only time she was not drinking. I hated payday and the weekends; that meant it was time to drink. That also meant a physical altercation could pop off at any given moment. I really tried to make sure I had access to a vehicle on the weekends so I could go to my sister's house and babysit to make my own money. I honestly think I would have watched her children for free because It meant an escape from the house.

One weekend, I believe it was Labor Day Weekend I'm not for sure, I was at the mall with one of my childhood best friends. We split up in the mall and decided to meet up later to make the trip faster. I was talking and I remember someone grabbing me by the waist and saying "Excuse me". See, they were doing construction in the mall and it was like highway construction only indoors. Anyway he looked very familiar to me, I just couldn't place where I knew his face from. He favored the character DeWayne Wayne from the show *"It's a Different World"*, I thought he was "cute". My pager went off so I was walking to the pay phones, I mean it *was* 1990. I saw him again. He walked with me to the payphone and asked me if I was on my way to call my boyfriend and I told him yes. He was actually a guy I had met at a club my sister and her husband got my other best friend and I into with fake ID's and it turned out he was not only older but possibly married. He stood there while I made the call, we talked after my conversation and realized he went to high school on the north side also so he rode the same bus that I did every morning. He and a friend of his argued with guys from my school almost every morning about whatever basketball game that aired the night before. We talked a couple of times and went out and we hit it off. He had his own car and he was working for UPS. He lived at home with his mom, two sisters, niece, nephew and his older brother. I wasn't familiar with that area of the city. One night we went out and we stopped to get a bite to eat. During this time of my life I could eat McDonalds **everyday** so when he asked me if I wanted something to eat, that's what I picked but didn't get my usual Big Mac with extra cheese and onions, large fry and coke; I got a cheeseburger, small fry and a small drink. We laughed about that often later on. We went back to his house that night and he lived on the 3rd floor. He had his own room. We ate, cuddled, and had unprotected sex. A few days after that their phone was disconnected. Again, I was not familiar with that area so I didn't remember where he lived. One day I just happened to be turning onto Jackson BLVD and there he was sitting at the light headed West. He was headed to my house. So we became a couple. During this time my sister was having marital problems, my mom was still drinking but it seemed like more than usual, and I was falling hard for this boy. My sister decided she wanted a divorce and she wanted to take a rode trip to Tennessee to visit our cousin and I would be going with her to help her drive. My father was very clear that my boyfriend could **not** go with us, but he went anyway. We definitely had an illegal amount of unprotected sex. I'll never forget he performed oral sex on me and when he was done he sat at foot of the bed and cried. When I asked why he was crying he said he had never done that before and he told me he loved me…

 A couple of days later our dad called and told my sister that he said he didn't want my him riding down there with us and he wanted us on the road 1st thing in the morning. Well damn. When we made it back my sister told her husband she changed her mind and no longer wanted a divorce. He said no. She tried to commit suicide. My boyfriend and I stayed with her at the hospital because they had her on a suicide watch and upon her release she was going to need a place to stay to start the healing process. This was my introduction to mental illness. My boyfriend and I went to my house one evening after visiting my sister and the house looked a mess. There was clearly a fight of some sort that had taken place earlier that day. There was a pitcher of Kool-Aid thrown so the floors were sticky with newspaper stuck on top of it. Furniture was displaced. I just sat down and began to cry because neither one of my parents were home so I was thinking all kinds of stuff. I started to clean up and my boyfriend helped. Turns out my father tricked my mom and told her they were going car shopping. They actually ended up at the Mental/Rehabilitation Facility next door to the car dealership. They were expecting him. Since she was combative towards the staff when they arrived, she was in some sort of a padded room initially. Even though I knew she needed the help, I hated seeing her in that place. My father did this because my sister was going to be coming home to stay with us and he didn't want her to have to deal with our mother's drinking and the verbal abuse that came along with it. He also used that time to redecorate their room so everything could be "like new" upon our mom's return. I can't remember how long she was in rehab. I do remember when she came home. She was what is called a "dry drunk.; very angry, resentful, and very negative all to the point where you almost wanted her to crack one open. She managed to stay sober for 6 months and I remember going to a ceremony where she received a coin and everything. I was very proud of her.

    My boyfriend and I had been spending a lot of time together and I ultimately found out I was pregnant. I was ok with it but I didn't know who to tell. I was 20 years old, I had spent years helping raise my niece and nephews but I knew actually carrying a baby and taking care of a baby 24/7 was going to be different. I believe I told my sister or my oldest brother I was pregnant but either way it didn't take long for my parents to find out. I was working at the mall at the time so for a few days I seemed to be able to miss seeing my parents. I knew they were going to be disappointed. The day finally arrived, he and I sat down together with my mother. He asked her if he could call her mom and she shut that down quick. She told him she was not his mother. The months went by, we found out we were having a boy and a baby shower was being planned then boom he proposed in the very spot where we bumped into each other in the mall. I said yes. It was very romantic and it was the happiest day of my life. The next day I told my dad and he told me I didn't have to marry him in order to have my baby because he, my dad, would always have my back.

    We were attending bible study every Wednesday and the pastor and his wife were going to be our son's God Grand Parents. We had an immediate family only ceremony at the church because my parents felt that it was going to become too big of an event and it would be better to have a reception four months after the baby was born. The day after we were married he lost his job at UPS. We moved into the basement apartment of my parents building. It had 2 bedrooms, a living room, a kitchen, and of course a bathroom. I had applied for a Medicaid while I was pregnant and eventually food stamps. We pretty much gave my dad part of the food stamps as rent. I can't say that he was actively looking for work. It didn't seem to matter because he was helping my father around the house and it was cool. My niece slept downstairs sometimes and that was cool; it felt like she was more of a little sister to be honest. I vaguely remember one night the cubs played what I believe was one of the longest played baseball games at the time. She and I were in my bed and I remember he kept coming in and out of the room but I was in a twilight type of sleep. I'm not sure how long the game went but he slept on the couch. The next day we were out and about, I remember being very tired. I also remember the house was very tense. We always entered our apartment by walking through my parents apartment and then down the back stairs. When we entered the back part of the basement, my dad was putting something in the washing machine and I heard him tell my husband that he had heard some things about him. I kept walking with the baby. A few moments later my husband came into our bedroom saying that my niece told my sister he touched her while she was asleep in bed with me; I was livid. I don't even think I asked him if it was true or not; a part of me deep down recalled the night she was talking about but I don't remember feeling the cover moving or anything. I kept asking myself 'why would my husband want to touch a little girl' but another part of me remembered me being that little girl. A few weeks went by and I managed to avoid everyone; I was looking for a place to move. The "situation" was never really talked about it just kind of "went away""; you know just like it did when I was a kid.

    Our church was working with Habitat for Humanity and they had a leasing office close to the church. We found a 3 bedroom third floor apartment for $450/month. I found a job working with the gas company and my husband would stay at home with the baby. My dad would pick me up in the morning so I could drop him back off at home and use his car to go to work. My sister ended up moving in the same building and so did my older brother and his wife. We all shared the same back porch. My sister's divorce became final somewhere along the way and our father financed it. She decided to give her now ex-husband custody of their two boys and that upset our father quite a bit. She couldn't really explain why because whenever she went to our parents house she and our mom argued. The post office was offering an early retirement to employees who had over 30 years of service. My dad jumped at the offer. He decided he wanted to have a retirement party, so we all planned it. His only must have was that a friend of mines at the time with a beautiful voice sing *"I Did it My Way"* by Frank Sinatra. The way the banquet hall was set up he and my mom were seated up looking down so they could see everyone in the room. There were so many nice tributes, poems, jokes, and the place was packed. He was in awe because the tickets were $50 each. My mom said he leaned over to her and said that seeing all of those people walking by and congratulating him and saying all those nice things put him in mind of a funeral. I swear he smiled for the entire weekend. On the agenda, post retirement, was a cruise to Mexico. Our parents traveled all the time. He also decided to buy into a neighborhood corner store/restaurant with a friend of his. He was also still taking my mom out to visit patients. I remember times we would be sitting on the front porch and it would be the weekend when my sister would have her sons or on a Sunday. My dad would ask what did they want to eat and he would go down the street and open the restaurant to whip up everyones order. His retirement was off to a good start.

Since we had our own place, we had friends over pretty much every weekend, Spades and drinking. I was not a fan of beer. I enjoyed having company over, there were couples but the guys were his friends. I still can't really recall him actively looking for work. I was still working with the gas company, I had just turned 22 when my dad retired and three months later found out I was pregnant. It was on pace, our son was on track to being potty trained before he turned two. My boss was actually a contractor who was hired to install devices onto gas meters that could be read from the vehicles instead of walking from house to house. My job was to assign routes to the guys, do payroll, and watch my soap operas everyday. One thing that really bonded my dad and I together was our love for All My Children. He and my husband also grew very close. They hung out at the local lounge down the street from the house so much people down there thought he was his son. He ended up closing the restaurant because his partner died and he said it was too much to deal with the restaurant, taking my mom to see patients, and still deal with her drinking. Now he decided he wanted to pull up the carpet and strip the floors and restore the wood in the living and dining room to its "original" state. I knew it was going to be gorgeous. That was a project that he and my husband would work on together. My father never stopped smoking after his heart attack 5 years before, he was sort of a rebel. He didn't like doctors, he only loved the nurse he was married to.

My niece attended school down the street from my parents house, so on this particular morning I dropped her off and she needed money for a field trip but my dad was asleep right there on the couch in the family/dining room so instead of waking him up I just gave her the money she needed. My mother decided she wanted me to drop her to our apartment and she'd spend the day with my husband and son because she and my dad had had words the night before. I was bummed because I kind of wanted to wake him up so he could see my t-shirt, it said "I'm Pregnant and I've fallen and I can't get up" it was funny at that time because he thought the Life Alert commercials were funny and not convincing (they still aren't when you think about it). Anyway, I remember she checked the thermostat and we left. I dropped her off and went to work. It was a normal day, the guys all received their routes and boss decided he wanted to follow one guy so he would be gone most of the day. All My Children was about to come on so I called my father to make sure he set the VCR or if he was watching because it was suppose to be a "big deal". So I was sitting at my desk, for anyone who followed the soaps it was the episode when Tad Martin came back. I called my father so many times so we could talk about it. I ended up calling my husband. He wasn't as excited as my dad would have been but he was telling me about how my mother kept saying how upset she was with my dad and how sometimes she wished she wasn't there when he had his heart attack. Had she not been there, he would have died. Well when I got off work my husband and I took the baby to get some shoes so we dropped my mother off at home. When we pulled in their garage it was weird because the baby was crying because he wanted to go inside to see grandaddy even though we were coming back tomorrow which was going to be Saturday. We went home and we were all hanging out at my brother's apartment because their apartment was in the middle. We were talking about the soaps, the conversation my mom had that day with my husband and just random stuff. My husband came over and said my mother called and said one of us needed to check on our father. I told them my husband and I would go over. When we arrived we kept knocking on the front door and no one answered. The tenants upstairs let me walk through and so I could go down to the backdoor. The house was pitch black. I turned on the light and my father was laying in the same position on the couch that he was in earlier that morning. When she adjusted the thermostat that morning, she was actually turning it down. It was cold and I touched his hand and I saw how pale they were but the nail beds were very dark, his hand was hard as a brick, I yelled out "Oh no daddy wake up! Wake up!" My husband was standing in the middle of the room and just kept saying - "Come on Mr. Smith man... come on" His best friend had road over to the house with us and he was just standing in disbelief. I went to my parents room and my mother was siting in the dark looking as if she had seen a ghost. I remember asking her when did she realize he was dead, because he was in that position when I got there that morning. It was as if she couldn't find the words. I called my siblings. The tenants from upstairs came downstairs and said they had been calling all day because it was cold and they wanted the heat turned up. I told them my father had passed away and apologized. We called 911 and the police, paramedics, and fire truck came. We were told the coroner would have to come to pronounce him dead and if we didn't have insurance or know which funeral home we wanted to use, he would be taken to the county morgue. All I could hear was my dad saying have them move the body the least amount of times as possible. I was sitting in his chair, and I was waiting on him to turn over and ask why the hell were all of these people in our house. I had got to a point where I could not catch my breath, I was 3 months pregnant. The EMT had to take my blood pressure and the only person whose voice could calm me down was my husband. We decided which funeral home we wanted to use and finally after what seemed like an eternity, the coroner arrived and pronounced him dead. He had passed away sometime during the night on Thursday going into Friday morning. The temperature was so low in the house that rigor mortis had set in but his body did not smell. I couldn't move from that chair. My father was laying on his right side facing the back of the couch and he had his left arm propped up on the top of the back pillow. He was wearing jeans and a grey t-shirt. When they turned him over they let me know they were going to have to force his arm down and it would make a breaking noise and based on my recent episode maybe it would be better if I stepped out onto the porch. I didn't want to leave my daddy by himself. The Pastor from our church was there by this time along with another couple. They were in the bedroom with my mother. Just like that our daddy was dead. I was prepared 5 years ago when they said he had 24-48 hours; but not like this. My mother was so strong, he passed away on a Friday and she wanted everything done by the next Friday. My aunt hugged her so tight and told her people don't realize how much they are asking of their undertaker when they have the body out so long and she stood by her decision. It was the beginning of February and we were expecting an ice storm. We had family coming from Tennessee, Missouri, California, and my brother had to drive up from Peoria. I wasn't able to go back into the house, it was too upsetting, but I picked the suit for him to wear. When I was pregnant with my son I bought my father two suits and I chose the suit he wore to his retirement party because that was the happiest I saw him. My aunt helped me find something to wear. My father always told me no black at his funerals and no flowers. He wanted his flowers while he was alive so he could smell them. His best friend had passed away a few months before his retirement party so we also knew were he wanted to be buried. We asked people in lieu of flowers to please donate to Habitat for Humanity. After all the details and planning, the evening arrived and yes there was freezing rain. My husband and the others had to get the casket up un-salted cement stairs and into the church; I could not watch. They managed to get the casket inside. I figured the service shouldn't go long due to the weather, we should be able to stick to the program. Since my husband and my father hung out together at the lounge so much, a lot of that crowd thought he was his son. I believe the entire Bulk Mail Center was there. My best friend came home to attend his services; that meant so much to me. After the hour wake had passed, I glanced around and it was standing room only and the church balcony was also full. People came out in that weather. My father always said he had been around the world once and shook everyone's hand twice. The Pastor delivered an amazing eulogy and she is still someone whom I call on to this day when I need spiritual guidance. It was now time for the final viewing and I didn't want to go up or touch him; didn't want to say goodbye - goodbyes are so final. My aunt was on one side of me and my husband was on the other side. I remember feeling like I was going to faint and I remember just saying "Daddy No! Daddy No!" My husband took me to the church basement, got me some water, and he just talked to me until I calmed down. I don't remember what he said but I remember my friend from elementary and high school complimenting him on his methods. That was a long night and we had to be up again the following morning for the burial. The funeral home was packed the next day. So many people wanted to see our daddy off to the very end. He had a 1/2 sister, I believe she had a learning disability but I'm not sure. She visited us 2 or 3 times and we never saw her again after he died. At the burial, she kept saying how he was her brother and I don't know if those were digs at the cousins he was raised with like siblings in Tennessee after his mom died but at one point she made, what looked like, an attempt to go in with the lowering casket.

Our father was gone, funeral was over, and the phones stopped ringing; life was supposed to go back to normal. It would never be normal without him in it. We learned from the mailman that my father had paid off the cruise he and my mother were going on and he saw him running through the race track trying to catch the last race the day he passed away. My husband also told us he had been complaining about chest pains and while reading the product label they were using to strip the wood - the windows should have been open and it shouldn't have been used around people with heart conditions.

> *"God has a purpose for your pain a reason for your struggle and a reward for your faithfulness. Trust Him and never give up!" - Unknown*

After the dust settled I realized our father was the link that held our small family together. Our father had the insurance in place on his car that stated in the event of his death his vehicle would be paid for. My older brother kept the car. My mother and I went to the cemetery to select a headstone. They offered her a plot next to my dad's so she could purchase a double headstone. As time was moving along I was getting as big as a house. My sister and

I decided to take my baby boy, her two step daughters, my niece, my best friend and my mom to the Mall of America in Minnesota. We were able to stop by the cemetery before we hit the road to see the headstone. We had a good time walking around that mall, well they walked, I was pushed around in a wheelchair. It had become too painful to walk and I had two months to go before our daughter was due to arrive.

    As Spring turned into Summer and as the mercury began to rise, I became miserable. At one point the doctor joked that maybe I was carrying twins. That's still not one of those things that one day we will all look back on and laugh at. My husband had received a huge settlement check from Walgreens. He was walking and stepped into a hole in their parking lot and injured his leg. It was during the same time my mother received a check from our father's life insurance. We purchased a new living room set and my husband took his mom furniture shopping; she picked the exact same furniture that we purchased. I still shake my head at that when I think about it to this day. It was also during this time when my husband became really close friends with this older gentleman that hung out at the lounge where he and my dad used to go. He purchased a pair of $1300 alligator skin boots and he also bought his friend a pair of boots, however I never knew how much he paid for those. When it came to money, he always "handled it". Even when I was the only one working we went to the currency exchange, cashed the check, and he put the money in his pocket. We kept our son in Nike brand shoes and that was all we wore as well. I wasn't into labels when it came to clothing,

I was never that way coming up as a child either. He bought all of my clothes and pretty much told me what to wear when we were going out also. I didn't really think much of it.

We reached our goal and had our son potty trained by his second birthday and before our baby girl was due to arrive in July. We threw him a birthday party with his favorite character, Barney. The kids that were there enjoyed themselves but my son did not want Barney to touch him; as soon as the party was over that rascal wanted to watch his Barney DVDs. July finally came and I gave birth to a 9lb 13oz baby girl. My husband was there during the delivery just like he was for our son. We named her after his youngest sister and gave her my sisters middle name as her middle name. When I was discharged from the hospital we went straight to my mom's house because I wasn't able to maneuver the stairs to the 3rd floor with the baby and our son. Our mom took our aunt on the cruise to Mexico with her. My feelings were hurt honestly, I really thought I was going on that cruise with her. She then decided to have some exterior and interior work done to the house; she had a staircase dropped in one of the big bedrooms into the basement to eliminate the need for having to walk out the back door and down the back porch stairs. The front porch was wood, the new porch would be cement. During this time our babies came down with the chicken pox. First our son and boy was he miserable for a few days and then sure enough baby girl came down with them. Everyone kept saying it was going to be better on us if they both had the chicken pox at the same time, shit not at bedtime. Especially not by myself because my husband had a nighty routine which meant that he went out every night to the lounge and he had learned how to play cards but not good enough to win. The holidays were coming up and it was only going to be the baby's first Christmas. It was our first Christmas without our dad; nothing about our family seemed the same and my marriage seemed to be like a favorite sweater that someone pulled the one of piece of yarn that was sticking out and the whole damn sweater was now a pile of yarn. Yeah, that part.

That Spring came and we moved in with my in-laws. Turns out several withdrawals were being made from my moms account everyday or every other day. She was given a description and it matched my husband. She kept asking how I could not know about the money and I explained to her, we didn't have a bank account because when we did he wrote bogus checks our of them so he could get the cash; whatever money we had in our marriage he had it on his person. I think it had something to do with not having much growing up, as I look back on it now. Anyway, we had a truck and some friends come by to help us move to his mom's third floor apartment. My husband and I were going to be sharing a room with our 2 children and a three bedroom apartment with my mother-in-law, one of my sister-in-laws and her two children, his youngest sister and every now and then his older brother would stroll in and stay for a spell. My husband and his youngest sister were both two strong minded individuals and they constantly bumped heads. Neither one of them knew how to use their words, so they had physical altercations often. It began to feel like the house I grew up in. My mother in law was a Home Day Care

Provider, I believe she had maybe five children assigned to her through an agency. The youngest sister helped her with the kids by preparing meals, setting activities, and I spent all my time in our room; our son played with the day care kids. During this time OJ Simpson was leading the police on a car chase on the highway out out in L.A.. It was in that room that I began to battle with Anxiety and Depression. Even though my husband was right there with me all day, I felt so alone and very disappointed in myself. My in laws spent most of their time sitting in the kitchen. I will say that while living there I was introduced to friend chicken wings with white bread and hot sauce, I was around 24 years old and I had never had the 3 together before. Lord have mercy, I was in heaven. I was actively looking for work because living out of that one bedroom was not cutting it for me and I felt like I was going to loose my mind. We went out once a month - the whole house; that was my mother-in-laws payday. As a couple, we did nothing.

I received a call back for an interview with Cellular One. The company was located in Schaumburg, IL which was a nice drive without traffic but I didn't care, I wanted to move. I got the job and after I received my second check we moved out.

"Isolation is an abuser's best friend." - Unknown

Cellular One by the way, is now known as AT&T. I worked as a Customer Service Representative in a call center setting, I really enjoyed that job. I averaged about 80-100 calls a day and eventually I was able to move up to Corporate Customer Service.

It was a long day of working and coming home and having to be mom and wife. I couldn't even begin to tell you where the money went. The place where we moved to was a two flat and the landlord lived on the first floor, she was a nice lady I remember her being very nosey. I used to carpool with different people, I met a guy who was very nice and he was a Mason. I knew my husband wanted to become a Mason so I definitely wanted them to meet. This particular day there was a bad snow storm headed our way and he offered to give me a ride home. What was normally an hour drive, was about two and a half that evening; there were cars stopped on the expressway because they had run out of gas. At one point they shut the expressway down to allow the snow plow and salt trucks to clear the road so traffic could go through safely and smoothly again. When we made it to our apartment, my husband was coming from around the side of the house and he was saying he had just been robbed at gun point. I was in a panic because after we established that he was ok I realized what was stolen was our rent money. I introduced them and they exchanged information, after he left I began to ask questions about the robbery. I wanted to know why we were not calling the police, I wanted to know why none of his jewelry was stolen, and then out of no where there was this burning sensation with a numbness to it. I think I was in a state of confusion- what the fuck was that? Then I realized my husband of almost four years had just slapped the shit out of me. Oh hell no! Who does he think I am? Who does he think he is? That slap was followed by a few punches to my arms. I believe there was a knock on the door, it had to have been the landlord because anyone else would have had to ring the doorbell. He walked out of the room to answer the door and all I remember was hearing him say was sorry about the noise and we would keep it down. I used that time to get ready for bed, I hopped in the shower and cried and cried. I was in total disbelief. What was I going to do now? Was he sorry? Who's supposed to move out? Who do I tell? Where do I go with two children and no car? Oh my God he just beat my ass! How are we supposed to pay rent? I finished my shower and put on some shorts and a t-shirt. I noticed my arms had bruises on them, I never bruised easily before but then again I had never been beat up before. Because of the snowstorm, our kids stayed the night with my mother-in-law and thank God it was the weekend.

    I woke up to him staring at me, before I could say anything he was apologizing while pointing out every mark he had made on my arms. He kept saying how he loved me, he appreciated me introducing him to my coworker because being a Mason would open doors for him as far as employment and things like that. I guess we had what is called "make-up sex". There was always a disconnect between us when it came to sex, he was very selfish in that department. It was all about him being satisfied which most of the time didn't seem to take long. For the first time in our short marriage, I feared my husband. I don't think I ever looked at him the same after that incident.

    We worked out something with the landlord as far as the rent money that was "stolen", then he decided he was going to find a job and he did; so now we needed a car. Our credit was horrible so he convinced me to ask a friend of mine to co-sign on a loan for a car and she did. He started working for Jewel Grocery Store at the warehouse, that job didn't last long before he got hurt again. We ended up losing the car and our apartment; we moved in with my sister and I was really beginning to lose it. We were sleeping in a room with bunk beds, it was a twin bed on the top and a full bed on the bottom. I was still working for the cell phone company, we managed to get another car. I went into work one day and I remember going into my bosses office and telling her I did not remember driving to work, I told her I believed I was having some sort of a nervous breakdown. I'm not sure how I ended up in the mental hospital, I don't know if I drove myself straight there from work or if my boss and someone else took me, I just know at that hospital I was diagnosed as clinically depressed and mentally ill. I stayed in the hospital for about ten days. I had exhausted all of my sick days and then went on short term disability and then long term disability. During this time off work I was seeing all types of doctors who were prescribing all types of medications that knocked me out most of the time. When it was coming close to the end of my long term disability benefits someone at the company suggested that I apply for my social security disability. My husband was not empathetic during this time, he would call me crazy and make me feel as if I were going to be institutionalized. I can't honestly say what was going on with my children during this time, I know they spent a lot of time at my mother-in-laws house.

We moved again, this became kind of the norm. We never moved anywhere and stayed until the end of the lease. This was a pretty big apartment. I was managing my meds and this was around the time when our son started Kindergarten. He was able to go to Lawndale Academy which was right across the street from my mother-in-laws house. He was a feisty one, he did not like school from day one. One day he managed to run out of the school and across the boulevard, which could be busy at times, and runback to his Fanny Bone house (that's what they all called my husband's mother). I was livid but everyone else thought this was funny. My husband was the disciplinarian, his method of choice was the belt…initially. Some of the spankings were harsh for the kids to be so young. I started having complications with the Depo-Provera shot, birth control, since our daughter was so large she had caused my uterus to tilt backwards. My doctor felt like it was best for me to come off birth control all together. During this time my husband went out pretty much every night, it was a process. He would lay his clothes out on the bed. If he were wearing gym shoes he had to take out to shoe strings and clean them and dry them with a bath towel and then use a tooth brush to clean the shoes. Then he had to give himself a lining across the front because he always cut his own hair, he would also shape up his goatee and then put on all this damn cologne because he did not shower. He would get dressed and say he'd be back. He went to different lounges and played cards and gambled with our rent or bill money. I could tell when he didn't have a good night because he would come in and pick a fight with me about the smallest thing. No one really came to visit us, no one really liked him.

After three years of being off of all birth control I was pregnant again. I had to stop my medications and I felt good about the pregnancy, I found out during my 2nd trimester that we were having another girl. My husband decided he wanted to become a Correctional Officer, the youth facility for the Illinois Department of Corrections was hiring. During the application process, I found out some new information about my husband of now 6 years, he did not graduate from high school and he did not have his GED either. All that time I assumed he graduated from Lane Tech High School but he actually got kicked out of there and went to Farragut Career Academy and just didn't finish. So the application required a copy of his diploma or his transcripts from high school. He took my diploma and utilized his art skills and *viola* he had a "copy" of his diploma. He got the job and went off to the academy to train. The baby was due Christmas, he was going to be done at the academy just in time to be home for her arrival. I went in to be induced on Christmas Eve but she did not arrive until the day after Christmas. A friend of mine was there for this birth and so was my husband just like he was for the other two. I didn't have a tubal ligation done right after the birth, at the time I wasn't sure if I wanted one more child or not. Sex had stopped early in my third trimester, it was just too uncomfortable. After about week four postpartum my husband was very horny, grinding was no longer enough. I was breastfeeding the baby in the beginning just as I did with the other two, I guess this feeding session and seeing my breast out was too much for him to handle. I put the baby down after she was done and I got back under the covers, he pulled my closer to him. I figured ok we are going to mess around until he cumms because I was not on any birth control and I had not been to my sex week check up yet to make sure everything with this pregnancy ended well. He had other plans. He was really into it, I found myself having to wrangle my way out of his arms, he was kissing me so hard. I was trying to call his name because it seemed as is he had zoned out or something. He started removing my underwear and I told him we could not do anything for another two weeks. He said fuck that. My husband kept a gun, which belonged to his father, in his closet. I never touched it, I didn't like guns. I never knew if it was loaded or not. I told him I didn't want to do anything until after my appointment. It was dark in the room, I could hear him open the closet door but I didn't think much of it. He got back in the bed. The next I felt was something hard pressed up against my head. I was his fathers raggedy gun. He asked me if I was ready... that night I was raped by my husband. I cried myself to sleep, but quietly because I didn't want to wake the baby. When I went for my six week check-up I was indeed pregnant. I was not keeping it. I immediately felt no connection to that "baby". I scheduled an appointment at the County Hospital. A friend told me it would cost $50 but I had to be there all day. My husband took me to the hospital and dropped me off as if he were a cab, he left me to go through that ordeal alone. I was amongst the company of young ladies who seemed to use to procedure as a form of birth control. They had us in a ward with 8-10 beds, I didn't have much to add to the conversation I just wanted it to be over. They rolled us each out one by one, I was rolled out into this cold drafty hallway. There were fluorescent bulbs that lined the hallway, half of them were just flickering. I could hear the vacuum sound from the abortion being performed on the young lady ahead of me, I could also hear her crying. It was now my turn, I laid there without any feelings or emotions in my entire body. When I was done I called my husband, he and his friend picked me up. He dropped me off at home and he went out.

> *"Maybe you are in a relationship and deep down you know the person is not good for you. You know this individual is keeping you from being your best, but you may think, if I make a change I will be alone. You don't want to rock the boat. That's why sometimes God will turn the boat over. God may force you to move forward, not because He's mean, not because He's trying to make your life miserable, but because he has such a great desire to see you reach your full potential." - Unknown*

My sister came to live with us for a little while, it was cool having her there because I was starting back on my medication and she was developing a bond with the baby that would last a lifetime. I was finally called to work for the post office. I had passed the test several years prior. I was working nights and my husband was working at the IDOC and was also trying to manage a lounge on the side. It didn't seem like good business to me if he had to take money from our pockets to make the lounge thrive. I was called stupid and told I didn't know shit. It was during a bad snow storm that someone ran a stop light and hit the passenger side of our car. The fire department wanted to cut my door off to get me out but my husband quickly stopped them in their tracks. They had to carefully slide me across to the driver side because I could not feel my legs. Yeah, he was more concerned about his car door. I was not able to stay on with the post office following that accident because they did not have "light duty" at the distribution center where I was working and I had not been there that long to accumulate sick time or anything. My sister had found her own place and of course we had to move again. I had decided to try my hand at home day care. This apartment was closer to my in-laws, our son had his own room and the girls shared a room. The living room was right off the kitchen which would be great for the day care because there was a clear sightline between the two rooms. We spent time and money at IKEA buying storage bins and learning toys that I would use for my daycare. My husband was spending all of his off days and spare time at this lounge that was called 5105. He liked to gamble, but I remember my father always said gambling wasn't for everybody because he, my husband, was not good at it and he could NOT be taught. He was still working at the Department of Corrections but he was starting to try to manipulate the system. He was using a lot of sick days for nothing, although he was complaining of some pain in his stomach the pain kept him from working but it didn't keep him from going out to the hole in the wall lounges. He filed his income taxes and when he received his return he bought an apartment sized washer and dryer, the girls got a nice set of bunk beds. "Things" never impressed me, I wanted his time. I was at my happiest when we were all wearing our matching Old Navy Fourth of July t-shirt every year and hanging out at Navy Pier. I enjoyed going to IHOP with the kids as a family and we would have a blast taking the kids to Game Works. I'm not sure when I exactly stopped being "happy", I can't honestly say it was right after the first slap or the first punch. I know I loved him but I don't think I was ever "in love" with him.

He purchased a black on black Cadillac Sedan and you couldn't tell him anything. You see, he was more concerned with how people in the street perceived him, I was more concerned with having a nice place to stay. I was getting so overwhelmed with him going out every night. This particular night, I told him I was going to kill myself. I remember he kept saying he felt we needed some space and he was gong to go stay with a childhood friend of his. I begged him not to go. When I woke up, I was strapped to a hospital bed with a bunch of cut marks and dry blood on my left forearm - I tried to commit suicide. I had also started self mutilating also known as "cutting". I remember hearing my nurse telling another to come look at my arm, I had my eyes closed so she must have thought I was asleep. I heard her tell the other nurse that cutting was "white people shit". I spent five days in the hospital and my husband did not come to see me at all, I don't remember how I got home but I know he didn't pick me up. I felt good, I felt strong. I checked the caller ID as usual and there was this woman's name on the the caller list. I didn't recognize the number, but it was listed several times so I called and asked for the name that was listed. She wasn't home. I waited and called back and asked for my husband and the child said he was also gone, in fact they were gone together. Oh ok. So, I had someone that I knew who worked for the phone company give me a physical address that went to phone number. Later that evening, he came home and brought the children over from his mom's house. We had words and things got physical, I was ready this time - I had pepper spray. No one told me I needed to shake it up and I didn't need to be so close. He ran out of the door yelling for help and our son and I were coughing because of the spray, someone called the police. Whenever the police were called he always mentioned being a Mason and they said "walk it off". Well he told the police I sprayed him with pepper spray and that I also sprayed our son. DCFS removed him and our oldest daughter from the apartment, they didn't take the baby who at the time was just about 1 1/2 years old. During this time, while DCFS was investigating me, I could not see or talk to my two older children, I was furious. I had one of my best friends ride over to the physical address that I had for the phone number. The lady and I had words on the phone, it turned out she was older, she had five children, he had taken our son to her house but told him she was a friend of his. She rubbed in my face how he was good to her; so I needed to pay him a visit. We drove down the block and I did not see his Cadillac, I didn't see it on the side streets and then my friend suggested driving down the alley - **BINGO**! His car was parked in back of the house.

I pulled along next to a garage a couple of houses away. I hopped out with a crow bar and I broke the windshield first, then I broke the rear window and then I carved random lines into the doors and hood. I heard someone yell out and I ran back to the car and my friend and I drove off. A few days passed and I decided to go by our apartment because I had been staying at my mom's with the baby. When I walked in I could see that a huge brick had been thrown through the large living room window, I reported it. The property manager, after viewing the security cameras, could see that my husband had thrown the brick through the window. The leasing office was going to give me time to move without penalty, they would just keep the deposit. He had already moved our daughters furniture from their bedrooms and gave it to this other woman with the five children. My sister had moved into a one bedroom apartment in Forest Park. The baby and I started going out to visit her when she got off work. She was such a huge help with the baby and a great listener also during this time. She never made me feel uncomfortable about the situation and that made it easy to talk to her about it. They say hell has no furry like a woman scorned, well let me tell you, I had a clear head since my release from the hospital. I decided to make some phone calls while I was awaiting DCFS to return my older two children. I called the human resource department for IDOC and I told everything. I told the gentleman about his fake diploma, the abuse in our marriage and the false claim that was against me with DCFS. The man wanted to meet in person. I agreed. He picked me up and I was able to show him proof of the fake diploma, he seemed surprised that it looked so authentic. He could also see that I just wanted my children back, he couldn't understand how the department did not remove all three children if they felt there was some type of risk of danger in them being with me. After our meeting he dropped me off to my sister's apartment, he gave me his card, and he told me not to worry about anything. He also let know he was a phone call away if I needed anything moving forward. That night my sister and I went out to this bar that was down the street from her house. She didn't have her boys for the weekend so I was able to go out with her and "relax". It was a nice place, I ended up striking up a conversation with this guy that worked at the liquor store that was connected to the bar. We talked as if we had known each other for years, he definitely had the gift of gab. He was light skinned, about 5'5 and on the heavy side, he was younger than I was. I was upfront with my situation, I let him know I was married with three children and my husband and I were separated all of about two weeks. He invited me to accompany him and a group of his friends on a weekend trip to Michigan, no strings attached. I thought it would be a good idea especially since I didn't know what to expect once my husband found out that I had told his job all of his secrets. Once I talked it over with my sister she thought it was a good idea, I walked down to the bar to let him know I would go on the trip. He was happy to hear my news and one of his friends that would also be going just happened to be sitting at the end of the bar when I walked in. He introduced us. He seemed really standoffish and bougie to me and I, for a quick second, had second thoughts about the trip. I felt uncomfortable with how his friends was acting and was wondering if the rest of the group would be the same way. That thought passed as quickly as it came. i came back to the bar one more time before we were scheduled to leave and I met his friend's girlfriend, she was a cute young white girl. She seemed nice. I met the owner of the bar and his girlfriend, the bartender and her girlfriend, who were also going on the trip, were there that night and they were very nice. I was now happy with my decision to go. I packed my suitcase with enough stuff to last me a week. LMAO! It was fall so I didn't know if it would be colder since we would be near the lake, or hot during the day. I just wanted to be prepared.

    Our bedroom had twin beds which was fine by me. Everyone was very nice and even his friend, the bougie one from the bar, had warmed up to me. We were on the beach one night, they had made a bon fire and we had some pretty good music playing. I realized the guy I was with was the life of the party and could dance. I was cold and his bougie friend offered me his jacket, I thought that was pretty chivalrous of him. It felt good to sit on the beach and just have a good time. It was something I had never experienced with my husband. we never went out together let alone with other couples. The next day we stopped at the outlet mall and did some shopping on our way home. As we got closer I was dreading having to deal with my reality. It felt good to get away. As my friend was walking me to the door, before I closed it, he told me he thought he was falling in love with me. I was not ready or prepared to deal with anyones heart, especially someone so young and someone that I barely knew. It was bad enough that

I went on a weekend long trip with him but he was trying to add feelings into the mix too. Ugh!

It was getting close to the end of the month so I needed to get my stuff moved out of the apartment. I decided I would move what I could by car and then get a small truck. I was unsure where I was going to be living with my kids, I had to think about rent, getting a job, schools, and my marriage. This particular evening I went by the apartment and I really didn't feel like going but I forced myself to go. I was startled when I turned around and I was face to face with my husband. He mentioned how I had been busy on the phone running my mouth, before I knew it he hit me, then I thought for a quick second that he could kill me right there in that apartment and no one would know I was there because I didn't tell anyone I was stopping by there. He started yelling for someone and then a guy walked into the kitchen. He was trying to get him to hold me while he took stuff from the apartment, but the guy didn't want any parts of that. There was a look in my husbands eyes that I am certain I had never seen before. I did not fight back, I yelled for help but I did not fight back. He didn't hit me in my face like early on when he first started hitting me. Never the less, the shit hurt like hell, every punch and every kick to my back seemed to go up three notches on the richter scale. A part of me wanted to die right there on that floor. I heard someone yell that the police were coming and he ran, I just laid there in the fetal position. I remember being taken by ambulance to the emergency room, they did x-rays and thank God nothing was broken I just had a lot of bumps and bruises. I called my friend from the bar and he and his bougie friend came to the ER. They went back to the apartment with me and he saw a picture of my husband and I on the fridge and was surprised.

He said, "Is this your husband?"

I replied, "Yes".

He said, "I would have never guessed he was married. He doesn't carry himself or act like he's married."

I was embarrassed but not at all surprised. I gathered a few things and we all left, I felt like his friend was totally judging me now. Hell I was judging myself! I took it easy for the next few days and I was able to get my things moved from that apartment to my mom's house. Slowly over the next few months a dialogue formed between me and my husband. His car was not running and he was now driving his girlfriend's car. He would pick me up after dropping her off at work and take me wherever I needed to go. I ended up taking over a lease on an apartment in a nearby suburb and the first thing I did was transfer the children out of the school by his mother's house. It was a one bedroom but we were going to make it work. The beginning was quiet, I had not lived anywhere outside of the city except for my short time away at college. I wanted to keep my location private as long as possible. I didn't want to deal with any unnecessary drama however I knew the police in the suburbs didn't play games when it came to anything. The apartment was on a dead end street and a grocery store was right behind us. I knew I could handle things for a couple of months but I was going to have to find a job. I was told about a job working at the front desk at the YMCA. I was dealing with some severe back pain stemming from the last beating I had endured. My doctor had me taking Vicodin at the time and I was still taking my anti-depressants whenever I remembered but to be honest I wasn't feeling depressed at this time. I was in some sort of happy place away from what I learned was a narcissist.

Narcissist - a person who has an excessive interest or admiration of themselves. They think the world revolves around them.

The crazy part is I still loved him, he was in my head, he was still playing those manipulative mind games. You know, the mental abuse. One evening I was in my apartment and there was a knock on at my door, I answered and when I opened the door on the floor mat was a night gown of mine and on top of it was a huge raw rump roast with a butcher knife sticking out of it. There was a note taped to it and it read - 'Am I My Brother's Keeper' and there was a Masonic symbol drawn on it. I immediately called the police. They came out like CSI, they took pictures and placed everything in individual plastic bags. I was a nervous wreck, my friend came over and so did my niece's boyfriend and they were prepared for whatever. I called my husbands phone about the package that was left and he laughed and put his girlfriend's reckless niece on the line and she made some idle threats and then told me to go take a look at my car. I didn't have a car at the time but I was using my niece's car, I went out to the parking lot behind my apartment and there another note saying the same shit. I knew I needed to defuse this situation before anyone got hurt, that meant opening up the dialogue with my husband again. He started writing me these love letters, telling me how things were going to be when we got through this rough patch. I have to admit, it all sounded good on paper it sounded like the man I married in the beginning. The holidays were approaching and the kids were going to spend part of their Christmas Break at my mother-in-laws house. My back pain was unbearable, I'll never forget it was a Thursday and I had taken the last of my Vicodin that were supposed to last me 30 days but here I was day fifteen being denied a refill. It was at that moment that I realized I had become addicted to Vicodin and I spent the next four days alone going through withdrawals. I made it through. God is good! I decided to ring in the year 2000 with a fresh start by finally applying for the job at the YMCA. It would be part time and I would be able to take my now 2 year old with me and put her in the babysitting room while I was working. Things with my friend were getting serious on his end so I had to end that, I don't know what he told everyone at the bar but I was not welcomed there for awhile. He had hinted that he was going to commit suicide and I let his friends know, but he didn't try anything. I cared about him but I didn't love him.

Happy New Year 2000! The world did not come to an end as predicted and I started working. I was dating, I guess, but I was still married. I had found about Cabrini Green Legal Aid Clinic and I called them to start my divorce. I didn't tell my husband I was filing, he filed his income taxes, claimed our three children and bought his girlfriend brand new furniture when he got his return. Nice! I was at the point that I was all too familiar with, the point where nothing really surprised me at all. Until one day my cell phone rang and it was his girlfriend. She called to tell me he jumped on her, the nerve of this bitch! But no, I was concerned and empathetic. We talked for a little bit and while we were on the phone he pull up in front of my apartment. She begged me not to tell him she called me, the nerve again! No, I agreed not to tell and at that time I did not mention it to him. I did ask what he wanted and why he didn't call first, he lied and said he was in the area and just wanted to talk. It was nothing conversation.

Over the course of the next few months, I was making friends at the "Y" and the kids were participating in activities there, I was even picking up a weight or two in my spare time. My mother-in-law, who I had lost touch with during the separation, became very will. She was always on a lot of blood pressure medicine but she developed some other health issues and was hospitalized. My husband was afraid of losing her, his father passed away shortly after we found out we were expecting our first born. My husband often told me how his father would leave home and be gone for months at a time but the last time he came home, he believed it was to die. His dad's nickname was "Pull-Card" because he was known for jumping from job to job. I guess that's where he got his work ethic from. I had saved up enough money for the kids and I to move into a bigger place. I had my eye on an apartment with two bedrooms, two bathrooms, and a balcony. It was located one town over on the fifth floor, I was excited about it. Then out of nowhere,

LIFE happened - again! My mother-in-law passed away, I had to break the news to my kids. Initially I was not going to attend the funeral, I didn't know where I would sit, the girlfriend and I were back into it. She had every right to be upset with me, I told her my husband and I were sexually active. I not only told her but I had dates and times and her whereabouts to back me up. I decided to attend the services. I was only going to the wake and funeral not the burial or repass. I was going to Great America that afternoon. At the funeral I sat a couple rows behind my husband and I noticed his girlfriend was seated towards the rear of the room. It was a short service and when it was over I went up with the rest of the row for the final viewing. My husband was bawling. I don't think I had ever seen him like that before. I hugged my babies, they were all crying. I went to tell my husband sorry for his loss and before I knew it he was hugging me and saying he loved me and that he was coming back. I looked towards the back and I could see his girlfriend abruptly walk out of the funeral home. As I walked out of the funeral home to my car I saw her off to the side smoking a cigarette. I was some what amused by my husband's outburst. I wanted to be a fly on the wall when he got "home" and had to explain all of that to her. I was all strapped in with my radio ready in the car. I looked up and saw the girlfriend standing in between my car and the parked car in front of me. I was feeling really petty all of a sudden, I put the car in reverse and when I pulled out of my park I pulled out but very close to her. I laughed and I could see by looking into the rear view mirror that she was pissed and I was being called everything but a child of God. I went on about my day, went to Great America, as a date, with a guy I had met and we had a good time. Later that evening my husband called to ask me about what happened when I was leaving my parking space. We talked about it and we actually laughed together which was something we had not done in forever. He started writing me love letters again, he was making a lot of promises. We came to an amicable decision, he was moving in with us. He was trying to figure out how to move the living room furniture he had purchased out of her apartment. She lived in a family owned three-flat. He was telling me he had to leave while she was at work, but I didn't want anything from her place. We decided to surprise the kids with news. It was a regular evening, the kids had just finished eating. My husband and I were sitting in the living, we told the children to come by us and have a seat. My husband took the lead. He explained to them pretty much that we were working things out and he was going to be moving in with us, they seemed ok with it at first. Our oldest daughter, who had never been good at whispering, walked over to me and looked me straight in the eyes and asked, "So he's staying?" My husband heard her and jokingly asked if she wanted him to leave, she verbally said no but her facial expression and body language said - HELL YES!

 I was approved for the bigger apartment and I was excited about the move even though I hated packing and unpacking. We moved so much our mail had a hard time catching up to us. I was still receiving my long term disability, but I had also began the process of applying for my social security disability. I added my husband to my YMCA membership, he would come there to play basketball and lift weights. Having him back, in the beginning, seemed like a good idea. He wasn't looking for work, I guess he woke up one day and decided to sell weed. That was not a career move that we discussed at the dinner table. The kids would come in and the house would reek, he was bagging the weed while we were out and I was certain if I could smell it in the hall our neighbors could surely smell it. The thing with voicing my opinion at this point was we didn't talk about what we were going to do *differently* after getting back together. I didn't know if he was actually done putting his hands on me or not. I just told him I couldn't have that activity going on because it made me nervous, and he just kept saying he wasn't going to be walking around without money in his pocket. I was still receiving my long term disability from SBC and was still working part time at the YMCA. He needed money to gamble with pretty much. My sister was getting married again, I introduced her to one of the guys from the weekend trip I went on and they really hit it off. I was so happy for her. They were planning to be married in their condo. One day I got a call from her saying she loved me and she really wanted me to be there. She said there were several people that did not want my husband in attendance. I totally understood that and had every intention on being there with my children. I let my husband know and he lost it, he lost it all on me. I remember he kept punching me in both my arms until he got tired. I got my pjs, took a shower, and went to bed. I woke up the next morning with him staring at me, I was also very sore. He was looking at my arms, at the black and blue bruises and was apologize for hitting me and for allowing himself to get so angry. I went into the bathroom and when I saw my reflection in the mirror, I covered my mouth with a face towel and began to sob. What had I gotten myself into...AGAIN?! A few days had passed and in the mail were court papers regarding the divorce I had filed, it simply stated I could show up if i wanted to pursue it or it would be thrown out. I chose not to go. I began to realize having my husband back had nothing to do with "love" or "family". I wanted to show that girl that I **could** get him back. P-A-T-H-E-T-I-C! I was able to hide my bruises because my sleeves on my uniform came down to just above my elbow. One day I was handing the bougie guy, who had told me about the job, some mail and he noticed one of the bruises on my arm. He didn't say anything and neither did I. One day he told me if I needed someone to talk to he was available, that was when I began to see a different side of him. He allowed my two older children to participate in the program he was running, he was a director. I'm not sure how he and my little 2-year old developed a connection but they did. She was in the babysitting room while I was working and he could not walk pass that window without stopping by and saying hello to her. He would give the older two money for the vending machines. One evening my husband asked our older daughter where did she get money from for snacks and she told him that he gave it to her. He told her not to accept money from him again. That evening I had to work, he offered her a dollar and she told him her daddy said she could not take money from him again, it was embarrassing. The fights at home were becoming a regular thing, I would pretty much just take the punches. One night I had had enough, I grabbed the closest thing to me, which was a lamp, and threw it at him. I also called the police. The police arrived and it seemed like they were instantly taking his side. I refused to stay and listen to the bullshit, I began to walk towards the elevator after after the officer instructed me to stop so I was arrested. I spent the night in jail. I was taken from there to the district courthouse where I was in a holding cell with women from all over the county who had did all types of shit. One lady knew right off the bat that I must have been in there for something domestic. I was released without having to post bail and was given some hours to complete in the Sheriffs' Work Alternative Program (SWAP). When I got back home I felt like the arrest was a game changer, I felt like moving forward that village police department would always side with him! They knew about the medications I was taking and the fact that I did not obey the officers order that night didn't help. I blew off the SWAP. One morning after the kids left for school there was a knock on the door. I answered and it was the Sheriff Police. There was a warrant for my arrest for not completing the service hours. We lived on the fifth floor. I needed to get dressed and one of the officers insisted I leave the bedroom door open while I got dressed. I was so embarrassed and uncomfortable. I kept asking where was I going to go if we lived on the fifth floor? Finally the other officer let me close the door and I got dressed. I was told they were doing a sweep and they catch people with warrants early in the morning. I had to pay $150 and that satisfied the SWAP hours. I think he thought I was going to allow him to just beat my ass from then on out and not and not call the police. It had got to the point where I didn't have to call, the neighbors were calling, I'll never forget this one day he was arrested for jumping on me and I had to go to bond court the next morning to see how much had to be paid for him to be released. The kids and I got to the court house and I was instructed that the court house was closed due to a bomb threat. I could see everyone was leaving from the building as well as the parking lot. When the kids and I got back home and I turned on the television I had learned of the two planes that flew into the Twin Towers. I spent the rest of the day glued to the television. My mom, who had re-married and was on her honeymoon in Florida, and her new husband were stuck because the US was on high alert and all flights across the country were grounded.

    My lease was now up and I had found a house for rent, it was the same rent. It had three bedrooms and there was a tenant in the upstairs/attic spaces. It was located in a nice area by a big park and would be ideal around the Fourth of July for the huge fireworks show. I was still working part time at the "Y" and the doctors were still experimenting with me medication. There were times were we didn't have food to eat but my husband would get dressed, just like the old days, and step out looking like a million bucks. I would page my friend from the "Y" and ask him to buy food for me and my kids and he would. Apparently, the guy upstairs was also the "look out man" for my husband. He told my husband that a guy in a white truck would pull up in the alley with food and would sometimes drop me off from work. My husband wanted to be respected and he wanted to be feared, he didn't do anything that would garner respect from another man and I had never seen him in an altercation with anyone outside of, his younger sister, myself and with our two older children. He could talk himself out of anything, he cursed like a sailor. The funny thing is when we were first married, several people said they felt God had an anointing on his life. Me personally, I felt that he had all of the characteristics of a dirty politician as time went on. He could lie, manipulate, and make me, and others, believe almost anything if given the right platform and enough time. I started seeing a new psychiatrist who prescribed me this medication at a very high dose. I had cut back on my days at the "Y" because the medicine was so strong and I was just once again in a very dark place. I had started cutting again. It was so dark and bad that I swear I was hearing voices. I remember hearing them tell me to write random words on our bedroom wall in blood. I wouldn't realize how bad I had cut my upper left arm until a couple of days had passed. They were very painful and I was very disappointed in myself for allowing myself to revisit such an awful "coping" skill. After about a year and half it was time to move again, we moved so much that we never received our security deposit back because it was never on good terms. I had found us another house to rent and my mother stayed with us for a bit. I was finally awarded my Social Security Disability and because of my "mental health" my husband was appointed as my payee. The way the money was set up I was supposed to pay SBC $13K for the long term payments they paid me while I was waiting to be approved, then the remaining $30K was ours. We did not have a bank account still so he decided to cash the checks at the currency exchange. His love of greed would not allow him to pay the money back that I owed SBC. We purchased new furniture, he went out and bought two cars one for him and one for me, both cars in his name. His wardrobe was impeccable.

The house was fine until he came home, our oldest daughter couldn't do anything right in his eyes, she tried so hard to please him but nothing was ever good enough. He wouldn't just hit her with the belt, he would open hand slap her in the face, it got so bad the one time she ran away from home and called the police. She sent to her friend's house close by and the police told my husband that he could hit her but not with an open hand in the face. I was at a loss for words. That was around Christmas time, and he removed all of her gifts from under the tree. That was a pathetic Christmas, we were at the point in our marriage where I began having an affair and he was spending multiple nights away at a time. The guy I was seeing was a gentleman. We initially starting talking on the phone for hours at a time. We didn't necessarily talk about "us" or my marriage, we just talked about life. He would pick me up after I would walk the little one to kindergarten and then we would go shopping or go see a movie. Sometimes he would get a room for us. He would always reassure me that I was a lot stronger than I gave myself credit for being. He helped me see myself different which led me to acting differently and caring myself differently. My husband drilled in my head that I was fat, ugly, and no man would ever want me with three children if we were to split up again. I believed him but I really didn't care.

I just wanted him to leave me. It had gotten to the point where I would call his phone after him not coming home for 2-3 days and a lady answered once and told me he was asleep and to stop calling his phone. Now I know I should have been upset for being disrespected by this unknown woman but I was not. i was relieved because she told me he didn't need to come back home because she could take care of him. At this point I knew it was just a matter of time before the inevitable would happen. I started searching everywhere to see if there were any money orders left. I had learned from the one Domestic Violence support group that I attended that I needed to have a plan. My nerves were so bad after that call that I couldn't eat. I was so anxious. I didn't know how he was going to act when he came back, would he beat me up for calling his phone? Would he beat me up because it was Wednesday? What? He came home and got dressed as usual, he didn't say much. He walked out of the room and then walked back in the room. I just knew he was about to kick off a fight. I was not in the mood. He stood at the foot of the bed and said "Dude I don't want to be married to you anymore!" All I said was, "Ok".
I had been so stressed out that I could not eat but in that moment I instantly got my appetite back. I went across the street to Portillo's and got myself something to eat. My girlfriend lived in a courtway building in the city, she talked to her landlord and explained my situation. All I had was $400 to my name, he agreed to let me have the apartment. We agreed that I would take the girls and our son would live with him. Looking back I know that was so I would have to give him our sons beneficiary allotment from my

social security. My friend helped me round up four guys from our old neighborhood to help me move. This was two days after he said it was over, I moved out of that house in 48 hours and I never looked back. I promised my girls that we would only live in the city for a year. We spent that first day unpacking as much as we could and all I was looking forward to was a good night's sleep. I didn't have to worry about him coming into the bedroom beating me up because he had a bad night of gambling. It was a calm feeling in that two bedroom apartment. Something that I had been longing for for so many years.

"And then it happens…..
One day you wake up and you're in this place. You're in this place where everything feels right, your heart is calm again. Your soul is lit, your thoughts are positive. Your vision is clear, your faith is stronger than ever and you're at peace. At peace with where you've been, at peace with what you've been through. And at peace with where you're headed." - Unknown

Made in the USA
Lexington, KY
02 January 2019